SAMURAI BULLDOG

SAMURAI BULLDOG
by Chibinosuke Dogizaemon

as told to

Jeff Hunter

with illustrations by

J.C. Brown

Weatherhill

New York & Tokyo

To Pepe, who taught Chibinosuke patience,
and to Ken, who taught him to sit

First edition, 1994
Published by Weatherhill, Inc.
420 Madison Avenue, 15th Floor
New York, N.Y. 10017
©1994 by Jeffrey Hunter
All rights reserved
Printed in Mexico.
97 96 95 94 7 6 5 4 3 2 1

Library of Congress Cataloging in Publication Data

Hunter, Jeffrey.
    Samurai Bulldog / by Jeffrey Hunter; illustrations by J.C. Brown. —1st ed.
       p.   cm.
    ISBN 0-8348-0305-4 : $9.95
    1. Bulldog —Humor. 2. Samurai —Humor. 3. Wit and humor, Pictorial.
    I. Brown, J.C. II. Title
    PN6231.D68H86 1993
    818'.5402—dc20
                                           93-40478
                                              CIP

Contents

Bulldog-dō: The Way of the Bulldog 7

The Arts of War 10
Secret Schemes of the Ninja Bulldog 12
Bojutsu: The Art of the Stick 27
The Ten Strategies 38

The Arts of Peace 48
Bulldog Zen 50
The Samurai Bulldog in Literature and Legend 66
Bulldog Haiku 76
The Book of Five Bowls 84

About the Authors 95

BULLDOG-DŌ
The Way of the Bulldog

The indomitable pursuit of Bulldog-dō, the Way of the Bulldog, makes the Samurai Bulldog what he is—expert in the Arts of War and the Arts of Peace alike.

Bulldog-dō (literally, "to let a Bulldog do what a Bulldog does") is also a time-honored discipline to which the Samurai Bulldog subjects his master.

First the master must perfect the Five Virtues.

Propriety means knowing one's place, and allowing the Samurai Bulldog to be first up the stairs, first out the door, and last in from all walks.

Humanity means allowing the Samurai Bulldog to sleep wherever humans do, including, preferably, on top of them.

Righteousness means taking up the Samurai Bulldog's cause when he is accused of persecuting a poodle or sliming a new silk blouse.

Wisdom is knowing that it is foolhardy to expect a Samurai Bulldog to go for a walk in any temperature over 75 degrees Farenheit, and that all compound things on low tables are impermanent.

Faithfulness means remaining loyal to the Samurai Bulldog even after he has snapped a prize rhododendron bush off at ground level in a heedless plunge after an imaginary rabbit.

By perfecting these virtues, master and Bulldog are joined in the seamless bond of collar and leash, walking as one on the Way.

In war or peace, the Samurai Bulldog never forgets the maxim, "Though a warrior may be called a dog, what is foremost is for him to win." He is serene and immoveable, for he has looked the Last Nap right in its face—and yawned. This is the Samurai Bulldog.

The Arts of War

SECRET SCHEMES OF THE NINJA BULLDOG

Hone Kakushi no Jutsu

The Disappearing Bone

Kusappe no Jutsu

The Mysterious
Assault of
the Foul Wind

13

Teki no Jo ni Takara wo
Hiding Your Treasures in the Opponent's Camp

Ninja no Ango

The Secret Ninja Code

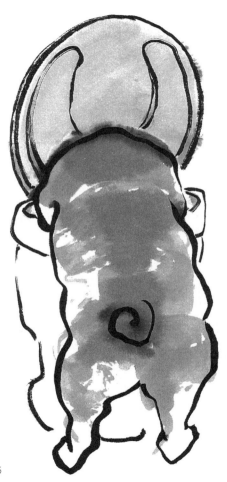

Mizupitashi no Jutsu

Drinking Deeply
from Your
Opponent's Well

Kakure Koromo no Jutsu
The Cloak of Invisibility

Sutekamari no Jutsu

Making Your Own Body into a Booby Trap

Nukeana no Jutsu

Escaping Through the Open Gate of
the Enemy Fortress

Hagakure no Jutsu

Disappearing in
a Whirlwind of
Leaves

Yodare Kake no Jutsu

The Flurry of Flying Drool

Onigao no Jutsu
Donning the
Demon Mask

Jutan Kegashi no Jutsu

Leaving Your Mark
and Fleeing
the Scene

Hyakumenso no Jutsu

Myriad Disguises
of the Ninja Bulldog

a.

b.

c.

d.

Key

a. Scottish
terrier
b. Cat
c. Collie
d. Poodle

A Thousand-
and-One
Faces

THE ART OF THE STICK

"The Stick is the soul of the Samurai Bulldog. He should practice stick-fighting every morning and evening, without fail. Only thus will he become one with the stick, perfect his art, and defeat his opponent."

SELECTING YOUR WEAPON

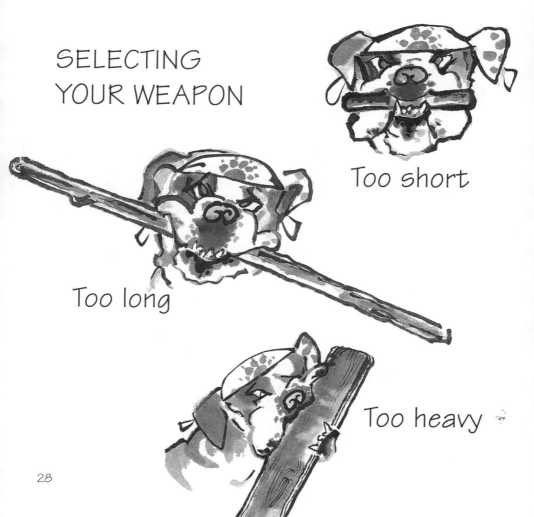

Too short

Too long

Too heavy

Too soft

Too oddly shaped

JUST RIGHT

THE GRIP

No...

No...

YES!

Benkei-zeme

Hitting the Bone

Nebari-odoshi

Menacing with Slime

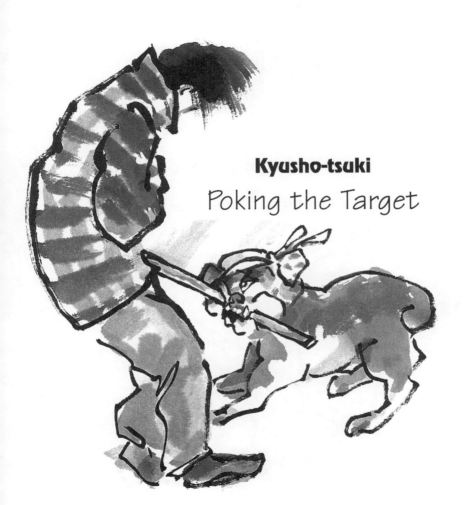

Kyusho-tsuki

Poking the Target

Nihon Ashi-oshi

The Biped Shove

Furi-furi Kakemawashi

Shaking and Chasing

The Secret of Ultimate Victory...

NEVER LET GO

THE TEN STRATEGIES

1. Feint east, strike west.

2. Sneak across the
ocean in broad daylight.

3. Watch the fire from the opposite bank of the river.

4. Hide a sword in a smile.

5. Stir up the waters to catch fish.

6. Steal a beam to replace a pillar.

7. Feign ignorance without going crazy.

44

8. Turn the guest into the host.

9. Scheme with
double agents.

10. It is best to run.

The Arts of Peace

BULLDOG ZEN

The Sagging Jowl Record:
Zen Lessons of Chibinosuke

Episode 1
Coming when Called

Chibinosuke was wandering in the mountains when he heard his Master calling him. The calling went on and on for some time, but Chibinosuke paid it no heed. Afterward, when he had returned home, the Master confronted him: "Why did you not come when I called?"

Chibinosuke replied, "Where anywhere is there a caller or a called?"

The Master smacked him firmly on the rump, and Chibinosuke yelped.

The Master declared: "The called who is not anywhere is crying to be called by the caller long come back."

Quickly say—

Who calls who when no one calls or hears the call?

If there is neither coming nor going, not-coming nor not-going, does the smack still hurt?

When you leave the Master, who has gone?

Come!

Pepe-bo comments: Chibi was smacked for not coming. If he had come when called, what would the Master have done?

Episode 2
The Leash of No-Leash

Chibinosuke was walking through the town when he came upon a German Shepherd carrying its leash in its mouth. When he returned to his home, he told the Master what he had seen and asked: "Why does the German Shepherd carry its own leash?"

The Master asked: "How many legs do you have?"

"Four," replied Chibinosuke.

"And what do they carry?" the Master further inquired.

"My body and my head," replied Chibinosuke.

"Drop your leash!" shouted the Master, flipping Chibinosuke over.

Chibinosuke immediately righted himself.

"You've picked it up again! Can the dog walk with no-leash?" shouted the Master.

Chibinosuke lay down.

Quickly say—

Do sheep wear leashes ?

How many legs do you have?

If no-walk means no-leash, is a walk a leash?

Where do you want to go?

Pepe-bo comments: By laying down, Chibinosuke put an end to the discussion. What will happen when he goes for a walk next time?

Episode 3
Does a Puppy Have Buddha Nature?

Chibinosuke and the Master walked past a pet shop with several bulldog puppies sleeping in the window. The Master asked: "Does a puppy have the Buddha nature?"

Chibinosuke leapt at the glass and two startled puppies woke up.

"No," he replied.

"Which side of the glass are you on?" asked the Master.

"When?" asked Chibinosuke.

"Let's go home," said the Master.

Quickly say—

How many bulldogs are enough?

When you polish the window, do you clean away subject and object?

Do you want to go home?

Is it Buddha nature or Buddha nurture?

Pepe-bo comments:
One bulldog is too many.
You can never go home again.

Episode 4
The Great Woof! of the Master

Chibinosuke and the Master were wrestling on the floor when suddenly the Master began to bark. Chibinosuke grew very agitated and began to attack the Master, who quickly pinned the dog in a half-Nelson.

"Let me up!" yapped Chibinosuke.

"Woof!" replied the Master.

"Where was my bark before I was born?" demanded Chibinosuke.

The Master released him and sat cross-legged on the floor. He turned his back to Chibinosuke and hid something in his hands.

Chibinosuke wheeled around to look at the hands. The Master lifted them from his lap and slowly opened them to reveal nothing at all.

"WOOF!" barked Chibinosuke.

Quickly say—

What would Chibinosuke have done if the Master had held up a Nylabone™?

Whose bark is it anyway?

Woof!

Pepe-bo comments: I hid the Nylabone™. It's mine.

Episode 5
Just Sit!

In a moment of high spirits, Chibinosuke tried to climb up on the Master's lap.

"Just sit!" said the Master, pushing him down.

"Once I am on your lap, I will sit," said Chibinosuke, climbing up again.

The Master stood up.

"Where is my lap?"

"Just sit," said Chibinosuke.

TEST
Should you let your dog up on the couch?

Reverse Chibinosuke and the Master.
Do dogs have laps?

Look at a sitting dog. Look at a sitting man.
Are they doing the same thing? What is sitting?

Pepe-bo comments: Heel! Fetch!
Lay down! Roll over! Speak!

TECHNIQUES OF MEDITATION

Single-Pointed Concentration

Returning to the Original Self

The Deep-Sea
Samadhi of Infinite
Bliss

THE
SAMURAI BULLDOG
IN LITERATURE
AND LEGEND

The Life of the Swordsman Bullsashi

Bullsashi defeats Lassioka in the moonlight duel on the reed plain.

He Who Treads on the Bulldog's Tail

Bullkei is forced to strike his master Yoshitsune to gain passage through the barrier gate.

71

The Forty-seven
Loyal Canines

Aso no Dogi loses his temper and strikes the villainous Lord Bowwownao in the Pine Corridor of the Dogun's Palace.

73

The Seven Samurai Bulldogs

Bonjiro

Akita no jo

Yoshiterrier

Heipoochi

Preparing to defend the kennel from
the marauding wolf pack

BULLDOG HAIKU

Spring

春

Field of mustard blooms
The tangy, burning scent:
Rolling in offal

Black river-bed loam,
The first green herbs of spring:
Mud across the rug

Summer

Frog trills' soft echo
The heavy air as dusk falls
A hot summer fart

Tiny acrobats
Parade across the floor:
Early summer fleas

Autumn

The sharp startling hack,
Kneeling like a holy man—
Barfing autumn leaves

Sleek doe and new fawn
Seen through bare maple thickets:
Venison kibble

Winter

Into the white field
Burns a shining gold jet:
Urine in the snow

Jet black winter night:
Rousing the entire household
Barking at nothing

THE BOOK OF FIVE BOWLS

"Remain calm in the midst of violent chaos...

...never forget disorder in times of peace."

The Bowl of Earth

The true meal cannot be obtained by mastery of the Way of Mealtime alone. Knowing the great by way of the small, one goes from puppy chow to kibble to gravy-style chunks. Because a determined mind seeks above all else to obtain its Proper Meal, the Samurai Bulldog must master the Way of Strategy. And because the Earth sustains all life just as the kibble sustains us, we call this the Bowl of Earth.

If you would adopt a succesful strategy to fill your bowl, you must follow these rules:

1. Pay your morning respects to your Master without fail; don't spare the enthusiasm.
2. If you would disobey, do it after you are fed.
3. Eat what you are given, and always look for more.
4. Know where the food is kept.
5. As a last resort, eat anything; you can always throw it up.

The Bowl of Water

Our way is the Way of Water. Without it we perish. Water flows freely throughout the universe. It is in all things. This is its hidden essence. But its essence can't be tapped until it takes form. This is its manifest appeareance, which exists as the ten thousand things.

Essence is interior and invisible; it is the water. Form is exterior and can be seen; it is the bowl.

First, forget the bowl; then open your mind and see the bowl wherever it appears. This is the secret caNed "Never-lacking Water." But do not be attached to the bowl. It is only for holding water. Water **is** bowl and bowl **is** water. To be a dog is to drink from the Bowl of Water.

The Bowl of Fire

Fire is warmth. Curl around warmth, and you create the Bowl of Fire.

Where is warmth to be found? In a lap, before a hearth, in the sun, wrapped around a comrade, on top of your Master.

Seek it out and circle it. This is the secret of the Bowl of Fire.

The Bowl of Wind

Wind is motion. What does not move, we call dead. What lives, moves. What moves, walks. Therefore you must walk if you are to live. Preferably twice daily.

You walk in a line. But never forget that your leash is connected to your collar. Your collar is a circle

that holds your head, like a bowl holds food and water. Sort of. When you walk with your leash and your collar, you are practicing the Bowl of Wind.

The Samurai Bulldog walks in a circle. Mark your path well, and you won't loose your way. When you walk in a circle, you pass the same points on every walk, but on each pass you see more. The Samurai Bulldog learns by moving in circles. This is the secret of the Bowl of Wind.

The Bowl of Emptiness

"In emptiness there is eating but no food.
Breakfast exists, the Way of Mealtime exists,
the bowl is empty."

About the Authors

Chibinosuke Dogizaemon is the pen name of Chibibusuka Mizutama-no-yama, a red-and-white Samurai Bulldog (AKC#NM259953/01) born in Missouri three and one-half years ago. He found a home because of his spotted left ear, his aggresive interpersonal communication skills, and in exchange for the promise to buy a penthouse in New York City —leaving him no choice but to become a famous author.

Jeffrey Hunter is a translator from the Japanese specializing in Buddhism and literature, and the one who made, but has not kept, the above promise. His previous publications include **Snow Country Tales** and **The Animal Court**.

J.C. Brown is a calligrapher and illustrator living in Tokyo. He swings both ways, having also illustrated **Zen for Cats** and **Zen for Cats: The Postcard Book**.

The "weathermark" identifies this book as a production of Weatherhill, Inc., publishers of fine books on Asia and the Pacific. Typography, cover, and book design: Mariana Canelo Francis. Production supervision: Bill Rose. Printing and binding: R. R. Donnelley, Reynosa, Mexico. The typefaces used are Revue and Tekton.